CU00806759

Coventry Tales 2

A further selection of great stories, poems and articles from Coventry Writers' Group.

Greenstream Publishing

Greenstream Publishing
4 Hargrave Close
Binley
Coventry
CV3 2XS
United Kingdom

www.greenstreampublishing.com
Published by Greenstream Publishing 2013

Paperback ISBN 978-1-907670-36-7
Kindle ISBN 978-1-907670-43-5
Copyright for this book edition is held by Coventry Writers' Group.
A catalogue record for this book is available from the British Library.

Table of Contents

Introduction

Ann Evans

Coventry is a city seeped in history. Despite the many structural changes over the years and of course the devastation of the Blitz, our city still stands proud.

Coventry is a wonderful mix of ancient and modern; rich in its diversity of cultures; intriguing and often daring in its styles of architecture.

We have our cathedrals, old and new which stand adjacent to the ultra-modern structures associated with our university. We have beautiful historic buildings such as St Mary's Guildhall dating back to medieval times, and glorious parks like the War Memorial Park where we remember those brave Coventry men and women who gave their lives in times of war. We can walk through Europe's first pedestrian precinct or tread the cobbled streets as our ancestors did.

It's hardly surprising then when it comes to the story writers and poets that we have here in Coventry, that there is never a shortage of ideas for writings linked to our city.

So it's such a pleasure to be putting together another anthology of stories, factual articles and poems which are all linked to the City of Coventry.

This is the 3rd anthology that the Coventry Writers Group has put together. Our first was Coventry Tales, which became the *Christmas Number One* best-selling book in Coventry in 2011. Our second was an e-book called Christmas Tales. And now we proudly present Coventry Fact and Fiction.

This long established writers' group is, like the city itself, a diverse mix of people, from youngsters to the more

1

mature; and from multi published authors to those who are just starting out on their writing pathways.

We hope you will enjoy this anthology of stories, articles and poems by the Coventry Writer's Group.

Ann Evans
Chairperson
Coventry Writers' Group

November, 2013

Saved by the Sherbourne

Martin Brown

It's almost two hundred years to the day since the Swiss,
worried over Coventry's burgeoning skills in watch-making,
dispatched their formidable navy in an attempt to put an end to
us, their great rivals. This poem aims to commemorate that
failed attempt; a strangely forgotten piece of our history...

Jealous of our watches,
our skills and expertise,
the Swiss despatched their navy,
to bring us to our knees.
"The way to take this city,"
their Admiral declared,
"is to sail right up the Sherbourne,
and catch them unprepared!"

And with his mightiest frigates,
armed from stern to prow,
he set off up the Severn,
the Avon, then the Sowe.

Bristling with cannons,
and guardsmen keen to fight,
manoeuvring up the rivers,
they made a fearsome sight.

But when they left the River Sowe
they lost their early luck.
For in the shallow Sherbourne
the mighty fleet got stuck!

The admiral cried, "Abandon ship!"
Each crewman heard his call.
Making off with ships' supplies,
they fled to Willenhall.

And there they settled down in peace,
and vowed no more to roam.
Marrying the local girls,
they made themselves at home.

The admiral carried on alone,
travelling as best he could.
He waded up the Sherbourne,
'til in the town he stood.

Where two policemen found him,
a wet, bedraggled stray.
They dried his clothes and gave him soup
and sent him on his way.

He got back home to Zurich,
to ridicule and shame.
His navy was disbanded,
and never sailed again.

The Sherbourne's even shallower now,
and no ships come that way.
And no-one's tried invading us,
since that fateful day.

Fact or fiction...?

Visions

Ann Evans

Whitefriars Monastery, Coventry, 1566

Friar John was on his knees, scrubbing the stone floors of
Whitefriars Monastery. The cloister corridor seemed endless
and his hands were numb from the cold water and harsh soap.

"You're slacking, Friar John!"

The Prior, Thomas, stood over him. "Make haste!
You're to greet our esteemed visitor along the Warwick Road
in an hour."

"Yes, Prior Thomas," said John, scrubbing harder and
shuffling forward on his knees. "Though I swear we're taking
more trouble over Prophet O'Donnell's visit than when Queen
Elizabeth stayed here last year. I doubt we could do more if
Our Lord Jesus Christ himself were paying us a visit."

He expected the sharp cuff around his ear and jerked his
head aside so that it missed.

"Less of your impishness!" scolded the older man.
"Prophet O'Donnell is admired throughout the land. His
predictions are legendary. We are honoured to entertain him."

Friar John couldn't stay silent. "But the Bible says not to
listen to false prophets. Should we not put our trust in God and
embrace the future – whatever it holds?"

Prior Thomas's sandalled feet were close to John's nose
and John saw his toes curl in annoyance. "Less insolence!
More scrubbing, young man!"

John held his tongue, although he wondered if Prophet
O'Donnell wasn't becoming too big for his boots. Local gossip

told how crowds gathered wherever he went. He would be lavishly fed and a comfortable bed provided. His bags would be carried and people would even lift him over puddles so his precious feet did not become muddied.

Somehow, John was not looking forward to meeting the Prophet O'Donnell.

At noon, John prepared to meet their visitor. His fellow monks gathered to see him off, as eager and excited as children.

"Be swift now, Friar John," said his superior. "Take good care of him. Let it not be said that Coventry's White Friars do not look after their travellers."

"Yes, Prior," said John, hitching up his habit and running across the fields and out towards the Warwick Road. To his right stood Coventry's three spires. He crossed himself and ran on.

Reaching the Warwick Road he spied a small crowd leading a donkey and cart. A portly individual swathed in blankets was sitting in the cart eating apples, casting half-eaten ones aside and selecting others from a basket, as if the supply was plentiful.

The Prophet O'Donnell! John waited for the entourage to reach him, then stepped forward. "Good day! Am I addressing the Prophet O'Donnell?"

"Indeed!" said the stout, red-cheeked man. He stared hard at John for a moment and then announced as if it were divine inspiration, "And you are from Whitefriars Monastery, sent to escort me safely there."

The crowd looked astounded at this miracle of foresight, despite the fact that Friar John wore the Whitefriars' brown habit and white mantle.

More people jostled around the Prophet O'Donnell as they neared town, desperate to know what the future held for them. John sighed. It didn't need a prophet to realise they ought to be returning to their work unless they wanted their livelihood to suffer.

His fellow monks were just the same. They gathered like bees around a honey pot.

A meal had been prepared and O'Donnell tucked into the game pie with gusto, pausing only to relate tales of visions and prophesies. He talked to his gawking audience until late, becoming louder as the wine flowed.

"Is gluttony not one of the seven deadly sins?" Friar John mumbled as he scrubbed the pans and plates later.

"Do not begrudge our visitor some food," said Prior Thomas, overhearing. "It's only bread and cheese he requires now."

John kept silent. If Prophet O'Donnell was a fraud, living off the hospitality of others, it would soon become apparent. However, the following morning John witnessed the man's first vision.

O'Donnell was standing at the Oriel window, precisely where Her Majesty Queen Elizabeth had stood last year to address the townsfolk. He looked to be in a trance. Then his knees buckled.

John caught him. "Sir, are you unwell?"

Red-faced, O'Donnell pointed frantically. "Look, Friar! Look!"

"What am I looking at?"

"Are you blind, boy? Those golden and red lights. What are they? Streaks of flame? Eyes? Eyes moving so swiftly they become a blur?"

8

Seeing nothing, John called out, "Prior Thomas! Prophet O'Donnell is seeing things."

Prior Thomas came running. "A vision! A vision right here at Whitefriars! Praise be to God."

John raised his eyebrows. Some vision! More likely O'Donnell was suffering a bout of stomach gases from over eating.

Later, O'Donnell gathered the monks together to talk of his vision. Leaving their work, they listened rapturously, hanging onto his every word.

Over the next few weeks, whenever O'Donnell wasn't eating, drinking or sleeping he was gazing out at flashing lights while everybody watched in awe.

"He's a fake," said John, one morning after prayers.

Prior Thomas cuffed him unexpectedly around the ear. For once it hurt, as John hadn't seen it coming. "Less impudence! Have you forgotten his prediction that our monastery will survive when all around is destroyed by war?"

"But nothing can be proved," John argued. "I feel he is taking liberties with our hospitality."

Prior Thomas shrugged. "Admittedly, he does have an unusually healthy appetite. And he is staying longer than expected, but... ah, here he is!"

Prophet O'Donnell seemed excited. "What a wondrous vision I have glimpsed! Gather round!"

As usual, food and drink were provided to fuel his story telling. John stood at the back, arms folded.

"You, my good friars, are destined for such majesty, I can scarcely describe it," he exclaimed. "I have seen the words Friars House emblazoned in letters of enormous proportions on a shining blue-glass tower, visible for miles."

9

The monks were astonished – and there was more. O'Donnell was drawn to a rear window. Everyone followed in reverent silence.

But his mood changed suddenly. O'Donnell cowered away. "What monstrous vision is this?"

Monks craned their heads to see. But there was nothing.

O'Donnell covered his eyes. "Tis the work of the devil." The monks backed away.

He grabbed the nearest monk and dragged him back. "See! See that monstrous structure? Look, are you all blind? What kind of building stands upside down with its feet pointing upwards? Tis like an enormous dead beetle on its back."

The monks shuffled further away.

O'Donnell became calmer. "Ah! I sense its purpose is for good. Tis only the structure which is abominable to my eyes. Bring me more mead, quickly."

Gulping the sweet wine, he gazed out again. Once more he groaned and shielded his eyes.

"Now what?" murmured Prior Thomas.

"Not possible! I see a ship. An enormous ship bearing down on us. Tis made of metal. It shines like armour."

"How is this possible?" demanded Prior Thomas. "We are hundreds of miles from the sea?"

O'Donnell looked blank. "A great storm must have swept it inland."

The monks went into a panic.

Old Friar Joshua began to tremble. "Such a storm would destroy everything Nothing could survive such a deluge. Tis the ark! The end of the world is nigh!"

Monks fell to their knees in terror.

Prior Thomas drew them upright. "Be not afraid. It's nothing but one man's imagination." He rounded on O'Donnell. "This talk of visions is disturbing my friars. Time, I think, to bid you farewell."

Prophet O'Donnell left that afternoon. Friar John walked with him as far as the Fosse Way.

As they parted, the Prophet O'Donnell said, "You do not believe in prophecies and that is your choice. But what I have foreseen will come about – one day. The words Friars House will be blazoned upon a massive gleaming blue-glass tower. Streaks of red and gold light will flash past Whitefriars Monastery. A massive building with its feet pointing to the sky will overshadow this city. And a gleaming metal ship will stand before you. And you, Friar John, you will be remembered. This very conversation will be spoken and recorded in a book of tales."

"But we will never know," said John, bidding the man goodbye. "We will never know."

Epilogue

Traffic along Coventry's busy ring road sweeps right past Whitefriars' Oriel window, day and night.

The glass-fronted Friars House office block can be seen for miles.

Coventry University's library, with its strange-looking ventilation system pointing upwards, was opened in 2000.

The University's Engineering building cost £55 million. Some say it resembles a ship.

11

Cuttings

Chris Hoskins

We're in the spotlight
light spotting in the city,

Injections of cash are whizzing round the arteries of the ring
road
with the bicycle for fourteen.

Dan dances his way into a pop video
And a rocker has thrown his rocks at a book
and it only took him four days.

Trading standards are doing an under-rage launch
for the over-rage of the past
And an MP faces a grilling
but we're not sure whether it'll be on both sides.

Coventry City football club blazes into glory
while MENSA does an IQ test to tell us things we already
know.

If you've got a story to tell
you can ring the news desk
or search for a soul mate that may have a soul,
but you'll soon find out.

A postie gets a prize of £2000.00 in a prize draw
and he didn't even draw a picture.

Writers boost a cancer charity
and we all go down to the woods for a teddy bears' picnic.

Michael wants to become a Greek God
as we say prayers
at the war memorial
and sing songs of peace
for twins we haven't met.

One Hell of a Night

Anthony Bunko

A door slammed.

My eyes shot open. My face pressed against the cold metal floor. Groggily I clambered to my feet.

Where am I?

Some kind of old fashioned elevator. The type found in a 1940s hotel in downtown New York. Four eerie-looking ornate gargoyles glared down at me from each corner.

Where's Jez?

I remembered being in Club M. My birthday. We drank shots, one after the other. Me and Jez. The place buzzing. He handed me three small purple tablets. "Happy birthday, Billy". He hugged me.

I popped the pills in my mouth.

The music rattled my body. The rush hit me instantly. My head spun out of control. "Jez." I felt the colour drain from my face. "I need air."

He wasn't listening. Ogling two sexy girls grinding into each other on the dance floor.

I staggered towards the exit.

Then darkness.

The sudden movement of the elevator shook my body. It dropped downwards. Fast. The lights flickered and then went out. I gripped the sides.

Everything stopped with a shudder.

'10.35 PM' illuminated above the door. A line of bright light streamed in through the metal slats like an angry man

14

looking for revenge. I readjusted my eyes. I stood, staring out at the inside of the nightclub.

A body stretched out on the floor. People stood about.

"Billy... Billy..." Jez down on one knee. "Wake up!"

"He's dead!" a girl screamed hysterically.

Everything in my world moved in slow motion. I staggered backwards, bumping against the wall. "NO," I cried, "I'm not dead... I'm over here... look... I'm here". No one heard me. No one saw me.

A large bouncer pushed through the crowd. "Call 999! Call 999!" he bellowed.

The elevator dropped again. This time '11.41' flashed.

My front room.

My dad, as usual, on the couch, flicking the remote of the TV. A stack of my seventeen-year-old birthday cards above the fireplace. My mother appeared, holding two mugs and some biscuits. They cuddled up.

Loud knock on the front door. A puzzled look between them. My mother got up.

"If it's the Mormons, tell them to bugger off," my dad joked.

I grinned.

My mother re-appeared, her hand over her face. Two policemen behind her. Jumping up, my father spilled the hot coffee over the rug. "What's wrong, officers?"

"It's your son, Mister Jones."

WHOOOOSH.

The elevator floor gave way completely. I toppled down and down, deeper in the darkness.

15

I closed my eyes tightly, waiting for the impact. Instead I landed softly on a thick white carpet inside a well-lit casino.

A man in a dark blue suit greeted me. "Hello Billy, we've been expecting you." He led me to a rather uncomfortable chair next to a very large roulette table.

A bizarre array of people sat motionless around me. All shapes, sizes, colours and ages.

A commotion broke out at the other end of the room. A tall, athletic man entered. He took the last remaining seat. An Asian boy, sitting with his parents and his younger sister, rushed over and asked the man for his autograph.

"That's Danny McBride," the Asian man said. "New goalkeeper for the Cov."

"Welcome, Ladies and Gentleman," announced the man in the suit. "Thank you all for coming along at such short notice." From the inside of his jacket, he produced a red rose. He handed it to a pretty but solemn-looking girl. "Tonight," he continued, "we have six spins of the wheel. Six chances to change your life forever."

"I feel lucky tonight," the old lady next to me said hopefully. "I've been coming here now for the last couple of weeks and I haven't won anything yet." A hideous sore had taken over one side of her face. I looked away.

The man continued. "We have thirteen spaces on the roulette wheel. Everyone will pick a counter with a number on it from my beautiful assistant, Angela."

Fourth in line, I waited. I dipped my hand into the silky black bag. Number two.

"Good luck." The old woman squeezed my hand.

I wondered what the prize would be. Perhaps like a game show. The winner sitting next to a conveyor belt, trying to remember as many objects as possible in sixty seconds.

16

"Cuddly bear, food processor, cement mixer..." I almost laughed.

"Counters ready?" the man asked. Everyone nodded. "Well... let's begin."

From out of nowhere, a drum roll sounded. The wheel spun anticlockwise. The small white ball skipped and jumped around. Mesmerised, I watched its every movement, gripping my number tightly.

"Number seven," the caller yelled out.

I stared at the other contestants. A rather well-to-do gentleman slowly held his counter up.

"Mr Long, isn't it?"

The caller nodded.

"Well done. Please go with our lovely Angela."

The blonde woman led him towards an extremely grand door at the far end of the room. Inside, lots of people milled about on a thick red carpet, with brightly-lit chandeliers above their heads.

"Wow," I muttered, "I want some of that." I crossed my fingers.

A new game started.

"Number one," the man said.

Brimming with jealously, I again glared at the others.

A small hand appeared from a baby's cot. Tiny deformed fingers clutched a rattle and the correct number. Angela unlocked the brakes of the pram and pushed the infant through to the winner's enclosure.

"Oh, what's the age limit to this contest?" I whispered to the pretty girl. She ignored me. Instead, she fiddled with the bandages around her wrists.

"Number eleven," the call went up next.

A loud scream scared me half to death. The mangy-faced old woman's arm shot up.

"Well done." I congratulated her.

She kissed me on the cheek. "I'll keep a seat for you in the big room." She smiled and hobbled away.

I prayed.

An extremely overweight woman in her thirties claimed the next slot. So large, she struggled to walk to the impressive door.

"Only two more rolls to go." The man grinned.

I gripped the counter in my sweaty palm. The white ball danced around manically. Bizarrely, it came to rest on four different spaces at once.

"Numbers four, twelve, ten and six," shouted the caller.

"What's going on?" I stood up to protest.

The entire Asian family got up, smiling. "It's us… it's us."

Sheepishly, I sat back down, I whispered to the girl in bandages. "Must be a fix."

She ignored me again. I watched the happy family skip merrily towards the door. I wondered what my parents were doing.

Crunch time.

The last roll. My last chance.

The wheel turned slowly. The white ball, more mischievous than before, bounced in and out between the numbers.

Number two. Then three. Then two… then… finally it settled.

"Trust my bloody luck." I banged the table.

The good-looking goalkeeper held his muscular arm aloft.

"Trust him," I said under my breath. "I knew he was going to win it. Bet he wins everything. Bet he's got a gorgeous model bloody wife and perfect bloody kids."

Triumphantly, he followed Angela away from the table.

"Sorry, ladies and gentlemen." The caller smirked wickedly. His hand hovered over a big red button on the table. "Bye!"

"No... don't," I cried.

BANG!

A giant puff of smoke engulfed the room. I opened my eyes. I lay in bed. Walsgrave Hospital. Nurses busily rushed around.

What now?

I looked across the ward. Most of the beds lay occupied. In the far corner, a television played to itself. I sipped a drop of water. Something on the news caught my attention.

The reporter stood on the side of a road. Behind her, a silver BMW, crumpled head first into a tree.

I dropped the cup. The image of the Coventry goalkeeper appeared on the screen. The caption underneath read, 'Danny McBride, 1988 – 2013'

My blood ran cold. I turned to the bed next to me. The girl from the roulette wheel stared back. Bandages tied around her wrists. A single red rose sat on the bedside cabinet.

Another image flashed on the television, compelling me to watch. A fire in Coventry City Centre had claimed the lives of an Asian family. The photograph of the little boy and his sister in traditional costume caused me to black out.

When my eyes opened, Jez and my parents stood over me.

"You frightened me to death." Jez barked, wiping the tears away from his eyes.

19

My mother hugged me tightly.

"Get off, mam." I pushed her away.

"You stupid idiot," my father grunted. He'd been crying. "You'll never believe what we have been through tonight 'cos of you, my boy."

Jez chipped in. "Yeah, it's been one hell of a night."

I opened my hand. The counter from the roulette game fell onto the bed. "You have no idea," I replied, peering over at the girl next to me. A weak smile escaped from her mouth. "You have no idea!"

What happens when the Zombies come?

A Coventry Apocalypse Survival Guide

Gareth Layzell

The prospect of the world ending is a scary one, but in Coventry we aim to be well-prepared. The guides in this series will tell you how best to deal with the imminent cataclysms that may befall our city.

This guide focuses on the possibility of a Zombie Apocalypse, and describes ways you can maximize your chances of survival.

What is a zombie?

Zombies are a type of "Undead" – people who have apparently died but have not yet entirely moved on to the next world. Unlike vampires and ghosts, who tend to be relatively few in numbers, zombies multiply quickly into hordes and have the potential to overrun the planet in a matter of days or weeks.

The Zombie Condition is believed to be spread by a virus, normally transmitted when a carrier bites a healthy person. Once a person is infected, their bodily functions are disrupted and the majority of brain activity ceases. The body begins to decay, while all conscious thought is replaced by the hunger to feed on human flesh, and hence spread the virus.

The virus acts quickly, with the time between initial infection and full manifestation usually being a matter of minutes. Therefore the virus has the potential to spread through highly populated areas such as Coventry in a matter of hours unless it can be contained.

Due to the effects the virus has on the body, a zombie only moves slowly and clumsily. Nevertheless they are a still a major threat and should be treated with caution.

How will I know if there's a zombie outbreak?

National news bulletins will provide updates in the event of a zombie outbreak anywhere in the UK. In the event of an outbreak becoming a threat to Coventry, the City's newly installed Apocalypse Sirens will sound and all electronic signs within the City will display a large Capital Z to identify the nature of the apocalypse that is in progress.

Local radio stations will be commandeered to provide further information and updates.

What should I do if there's an outbreak?

The priority for the populace is to evacuate the affected area as quickly as possible in a calm, coordinated and above all safe manner. Where possible, the emergency services and the military will assist with evacuation but in the event of a severe outbreak they may not be on hand to help you. Therefore it is important to have your own evacuation plan in place.

Your evacuation plan should be simple and easy to remember. Make sure that all members of your family know planned rendezvous points. Be prepared to adapt your plan depending on where the outbreak is centred.

Your plan should also take account of the following:

- In the event of a major outbreak, fuel rationing will be enforced. For further details of how fuel rationing will work, see the Coventry Apocalypse Survival Guide "What Happens When The Oil Runs Out?"

- Rail services will not stop in any area known to be affected by an outbreak. Take particular care in the vicinity of rail lines, as train drivers will assume that anyone on the tracks is a zombie and will not slow down or stop.

- In the event that a large zombie horde is swarming towards Coventry, the Ring Road will be fortified as a perimeter. It will not be possible for you to move from within the Ring Road to outside it or vice versa. Similarly if an outbreak begins within the City the Ring Road will be fortified to contain it.

Remember that the zombie virus takes effect quickly, and be ready to abandon or dispatch your loved ones if they are bitten.

What should I do if I can't evacuate?

If your evacuation plan fails, you are advised to stay indoors until the all-clear is given.

24

Where possible do not congregate in large groups, regardless of how safe you may feel doing so. Large groups are more likely to attract zombies and, in addition, the larger the group, the greater the risk that someone in it has already been bitten.

Avoid large buildings such as the Cathedral or the Ricoh Stadium. Such buildings may provide the illusion of safety for large groups of people, but it will only take one zombie bite to compromise the safety of everyone inside. Furthermore, do not assume that the Cathedral, churches, or other religious buildings are automatically safe. Zombies are not known to avoid or be repelled by Holy Ground.

If you are caught outside in the vicinity of zombies, you are advised to move away as fast as you can. The faster you move, the less likely you are to be mistaken for a zombie by any armed personnel. Do not attempt to approach or assist armed personnel unless specifically asked to do so.

How can I fight off zombies?

You are advised not to engage zombies in combat unless absolutely necessary. Most of the time it should be possible to evade zombies without having to resort to such measures.

If you are cornered and have no choice but to fight, your priority should always be making sure you do not get bitten. Escape may be desirable but "cornered and safe" is better than "free and infected".

Zombies may be killed either by one of two methods:

Decapitation
Any one of a number of household implements may be suitable for the job — spade, meat cleaver, chainsaw, broadsword, scythe, etc.

Immolation
In the unlikely event that you have suitable materials and/or equipment at your disposal, destroying the zombies with fire is both quick and effective.

HEALTH AND SAFETY

Children should not attempt to set fire to zombies without proper adult supervision.

Remove Zombie corpses from your vicinity (or remove yourself from theirs) as soon as possible in case they have not been properly dispatched.

What should I do if I get bitten?

If you are unfortunate enough to be bitten by a Zombie, the simplest solution is that you *do the decent thing*.

Alternatively, you can make yourself known at the nearest military checkpoint. In the unlikely event that a cure is available, it will be administered. In all other cases, the military personnel will be as sympathetic as possible, and will do their best to make the inevitable outcome quick and painless.

Do not, under any circumstances, pretend that the bite never happened or assume that you will recover. Your inaction will in all likelihood put other people at risk and prolong the zombie outbreak unnecessarily.

Where can I find out more?

This Apocalypse Survival Guide summarises the most important information about the potential Zombie Apocalypse, but additional reading can be found in the "Armageddon Corner" of all Coventry libraries. Printed copies of this guide in a variety of languages will also be available. Audio versions of all guides will be provided on request.

This guide and the additional reading are also available online. Visit www.apocalypse.gov.uk/coventry.

Thank you for reading. Your diligent preparation for the end of humanity is appreciated. Stay safe.

The Coventry Apocalypse Survival Guides:

What Happens When The Oil Runs Out?

What Happens When The Bomb Drops?[1]

What Happens When The Sea Levels Rise?

What Happens When The Zombies Come?

What Happens When The Aliens Attack?

What Happens When The Meteor Strikes?

www.apocalypse.gov.uk/coventry

---

[1]Previously published as "Protect And Survive"

28

Inferno

John Sutton

Jack Pendle was considered a bit crazy by his friends. It all started when one night he couldn't sleep, went downstairs and started watching the television. They put on a documentary about the numerous ways human civilisation could end. Too tired to think about whether it was appropriate fare for someone with even a minor case of insomnia, he watched it anyway. By the time it finished, his chances of getting back to sleep had dropped from "a bit dodgy" to "you're kidding, right?" From that night on, he became obsessed with trying to prepare for the end. But there were so many ways it could happen! Supervolcanos, megatsunamis, global pandemics, nuclear war, alien invasion, huge meteorites; even climate change could cause ecological collapse, crop failure, mass starvation! How could he possibly prepare for them all?

When the end did come, it was on a rather smaller scale than Jack expected.

Most asteroids were made of (mostly) rock, but this one had been part of the core of a (now shattered) microplanetoid, and was consequently made mostly of iron and nickel. A passing comet was big enough to gravitationally dislodge it from its parking orbit in the asteroid belt, and sent it slightly too close to Jupiter, which in turn slingshotted it into a collision course with the Earth. It wasn't a planet killer by any stretch of the imagination – at about 150 metres across, it would barely be a pockmark in Earth's history, but it was still more than enough to end Jack's world.

No one knew of the asteroid's existence until it obliterated a satellite on its way in, and by then it was far too late. From the ground, the glow of the fireball was seen even through the thick clouds. People looked up, trying to work out what it could be, then someone got lucky and glimpsed it through a crack in the clouds. Even then, they didn't really know what it was (especially since it was already well on its way to breaking up by then). Jack, however, had studied up on these things, and immediately assumed the worst.

Some people had heard of the Chelyabinsk meteorite, and huddled inside, but not Jack. From the movement (and rapidly increasing size) of the glow, it was clearly going to hit much closer than the Chelyabinsk impact. He could even end up right inside the fireball, and he knew his chances of survival were remote at best if that happened. Still, he had to try, and he had to hope. Waiting indoors was futile – even if he wasn't inside the fireball, there was no way the house could remain standing through the air blast. He grabbed his medical pack, ran out into the garden, picked the far side from where the glow was heading, rolled up into a ball around the medical pack with his back closest to the house, and prayed for the first time in years.

Despite the amount of iron in it, the asteroid was too small to survive the fall to Earth intact. However, there was no time for it to fully disintegrate – instead, the fragments rained down over an area some 400m by 275m, centred some 2km from Jack's house. At the moment of impact, they were travelling at some 20km/sec, with a combined impact energy of well over 600 megatons of TNT, over 12 times the power of the biggest thermonuclear bomb ever detonated.

The first thing Jack became aware of when he finally recovered consciousness was wetness on his hand. Unable to concentrate, unwilling to unfold yet, he did the first test he could think of. He licked it. It was sticky and salty. Blood. Probably his, since no one else had been around. He couldn't afford to bleed out, so he tried to unfold, to check. His muscles wouldn't cooperate. He tried again and made a bit of progress. Good, not paralysed after all. Then light came into his eyes again and he looked up at the sky. Was it really on fire or was there blood in his eyes? That was only of secondary interest right now, though. What really was important was all the debris still raining down and, in particular, the chunk of (possibly red hot) rock tumbling straight towards him. Frantic, he half dragged, half rolled himself out of the way.

For several minutes, he lay there, wondering why he didn't hear the rock hit the ground right next to him and looking up to make sure no more debris was coming for him. There wasn't, fortunately. Then it began to thin out, giving him the chance to check how bad his injuries really were. The blood had come from a jagged shard of metal embedded in his leg. He could cope with that. What was of far greater concern was the fact that he couldn't feel his back or either of his legs at all. He examined the charred remains of his clothes, and any exposed skin. He saw to his horror that any patches of skin exposed to the outside were... wrong. Everything about them was wrong. The colour... even the texture, was dry and leathery, not like skin at all. Instantly, his mind flicked back to his research. Dry, leathery brown skin meant third-degree burns and life-threatening injuries. Clearly, he had been caught in the fireball, but had (barely) survived.

Maybe it would have been more merciful if he had died. He extinguished that thought immediately. There was no way a

31

planet killer would have let him live, this close to ground zero, and there was no way he would die to anything less. He couldn't have survived being spat all the way out of the crater, so he must still be inside. He needed to get out. He looked around for any landmarks, but saw nothing but utter desolation. It was as if the blast had chewed everything up and spat it all out again (him included).

Still, he had other ways to know where to go. He felt the ground and tried to work out which direction the vibrations were coming from. The damage should be spreading out from ground zero, so that way should lead to the crater rim. He bandaged up his numerous cuts and bruises, steeled himself, dragged himself up, went straight down again (his leg didn't feel right at all – one more thing to ignore). Then he sighed to himself and started the long crawl.

Two weeks later, two volunteers (Mark and Emily, by name), stood outside the 4200m wide, 450m deep crater and glanced around at the destruction. Even outside the crater itself, everything for miles had been levelled. Even in Birmingham, the glass had shattered. Still, they knew their jobs. They peered over the rim, down into the crater. Surprisingly, there was a corpse, about two thirds of the way down. They could almost imagine the person trying futilely to climb up, but that wasn't likely – almost certainly they had died on impact. It was a shame, but the body still needed to be disposed of. They set up ropes and harnesses and climbed down to get it.

On the way back up, however, Emily noticed that some of the bandages were surprisingly fresh, too recent to be pre-impact. They checked Jack over and, to their surprise, a barely detectable pulse was found. An air ambulance got him to the refugee camp, where they fought to save his life. Third-degree burns over 40% of his body (particularly the kneecaps – had he been crawling on red hot rock?), a broken leg, multiple severe lacerations, several serious infections, some internal bleeding (ironically, the weak pulse may have saved his life – the blood wasn't pumping into the injury as rapidly as it normally would), and severe hearing loss from the blast. They all wondered how close he had been to the impact and how he had survived at all, but they weren't going to let him fail at the last hurdle.

Three years later, Jack was just another badly scarred figure with barely any hearing, living all the way over in Leeds. He read the paper as he rested his feet in a bowl of water. There were rumours that they were planning to rebuild Coventry. Good luck to them – everyone could do with the extra space, if nothing else. Still, life would go on, one way or the other.

His feelings about the impact were more mixed than most survivors. After all, most had lost everything. To be fair, he had too, but he had gained as well. Very few people that close to ground zero had survived, and he enjoyed the gawps when he told someone in the pub about it. More importantly, though – if it wasn't for his long recuperation at the camp, he wouldn't have met his wife-to-be, Beth – the one person who saw more in him than just a victim.

A Coventry Immigrant

Anna Poynter

Leaving your home for the first time
is difficult at any age,
but when you know it will be a lifetime
the heart feels an outrage.

Why, when it is peacetime,
does your country feel like a cage?
For many years after the wartime
a neighbouring country caused that stage.

Whoever can earn strong currency by emigrating
leaves, tries freedom, rarely goes back.
Learns to live the foreigners' life: hard working,
unseen, avoiding flak.

It takes time to adjust to a new way of life;
however empty and lonely, nobody must have a clue.
Family and friends, back home together, want no strife,
especially from you.

You try to keep busy to assuage
the ache in your heart, then you hear a chime
in your mind of the sounds from the teenage
years you had taken for granted until this time.

Eventually you find your place in that foreign land,
learn to live the life of an alien, lose your innocence,
find friends to give you a helping hand;
You develop a new outlook and confidence.

You do what you had never planned;
you drop any grievance and become happy in your new
homeland.

Clara

Maxine Burns

Clara got off the bus, stretched, rubbed her large belly and smiled as the little feet kicked. She covered her mouth with a hanky. It had been over a month since the Blitz, but the air still tasted rank. There was a smell reminiscent of bonfire night from the fires spontaneously erupting amongst the ruins of shops, pubs and Coventry's great, devastated cathedral.

"Come on, Cyril, get a move on," she said, lifting her suitcase. They hurried along, avoiding other pedestrians who appeared suddenly, wraithlike in the smoky smog. Glazed eyes looked past them, of people silent and shocked at what had happened to their beautiful city.

Clara and Cyril walked past the Hippodrome, towards Lady Herbert's Gardens and the remains of the old city wall, arriving at last at Auntie May's pub, The Hounds of Hell. Clara shivered. What a horrible name for a pub!

They stepped into the gloomy, deserted bar. The air was thick and smelt musty, and a layer of dust covered the tables and chairs. Their feet left ghostly prints as they passed through to Auntie May's living quarters.

"Clara, dear!" cried May, hurrying over to administer a big hug. "I'm so glad you're here. Let's have a look at you." She held Clara at arm's length, noticed her belly and faltered. "Oh, you poor thing. You must be feeling dreadful. You're not to worry, I'll look after you."

She beamed, lit the gas and put the kettle on. "Sit down, you must be parched –

36

I know I am. Though there's not much tea, and you can't get sugar for love or money."

Clara twisted her lips and attempted to smile for her large, warm auntie. The smile felt odd on her face. Wrong. She turned to Cyril, who was standing awkwardly in the doorway. "Come on, Cyril. Say hello to Auntie, sit beside me." She pulled up a chair and patted the seat.

May hesitated, glanced at Clara with a puzzled frown and put some custard creams onto a plate. "Help yourself, love," she said, "then we'll go upstairs and I'll show you your room."

Clara stared at the teacups and looked up at May. "There's only two cups here, where's Cyril's?" she asked angrily. "And you haven't even acknowledged him yet."

"But Clara..." May stammered, the smile freezing on her face. She quickly put another cup onto the table and turned away, shocked to the core.

Clara sat on the bed and inspected the room. It was small but nicely decorated. It hadn't taken long to unpack, as little had survived the devastating bombing which had killed her family. She had been lucky, walking to the offie for Cyril's cigarettes. The errand had saved her life.
She leaned against Cyril. "This will do us for now, won't it? I can't believe Auntie was so rude to you, but she'll come round and let you stay, I know she will. You can help in the pub, do odd jobs. She must be lonely, rattling around on her own."

Cyril hugged her and placed his cool hand on her belly.

May was in the kitchen, peeling potatoes for dinner. Clara watched, tapping her fingers on the table nervously. She wanted to talk about Cyril, sort out the arrangements.

37

Before she could speak, May sat next to her, put an arm around her shoulders and squeezed. "I can't imagine how you must be feeling," she said. "You've lost such a lot. It must be so painful but you've got me – and that little one." She nodded at Clara's stomach. "He or she will make a big difference."

Clara yanked her arm away, stood up and started to pace the kitchen. "But what about Cyril? You've still not mentioned him. Please, Auntie, I must have him with me. I need him." She held her breath and waited for an answer.

May looked at her niece, at a loss as to what to say. "Clara, I'm so sorry," she eventually said softly.

"Don't," said Clara, raising her hand. "Don't say another word." Tears trickled down her cheeks.

May took a step. "But Clara –"

Clara jumped back. "I'm sorry I asked," she shouted. "I'll tell Cyril to look for lodgings – for both of us. I thought we could all live together, be a happy family. I was wrong." She burst into tears, ran out of the kitchen and up to her room.

May flinched as the bedroom door slammed. She stood for some time, stunned. She could smell the potatoes burning, but was unable to move. How on earth was she going help Clara?

Clara sat on the bed and tried to curb her rage. It wasn't good for the baby. She took deep breaths – in, out, in. They had tried so hard, helping in the pub. Laughing with the customers. Showing Auntie how helpful they would be.

"I think she's jealous of our love, Cyril," she said. "She wants me and our baby all to herself." She knelt at his feet and took comfort from his gentle hands stroking her hair.

The weeks leading up to Christmas were busy. Clara was a hard worker and popular with the regulars, who indulged her

38

fantasy regarding Cyril. May wasn't sure this was good for her. There had been no more talk of leaving. Clara was often tearful and touchy but, given all she had been through, this was understandable.

Tonight, Christmas Eve, the pub had been packed, everyone in a jolly mood, singing and looking forward to a good Christmas Day. But Clara had been particularly sulky and rude to a customer, and was getting on May's nerves.

"Get yourself to bed, girl, have a good night's sleep. I hope you're in a better mood tomorrow," May said, shooing her off.

Now, with the pub closed, May poured herself a large port and sipped it, relishing the drink and the quiet, equally.

They would have a good day tomorrow. May had dipped into her savings, buying new clothes and treats for Clara. They would talk; help Clara come to terms with her terrible losses. May took another sip. She must make Clara realize that Cyril was dead. Killed by that Luftwaffe bomb, dropped on its way back to Germany after the Coventry Blitz. Cyril could never live here, or help in the pub.

She would help Clara begin anew. This New Year would be a fresh start for them both.

May finished her drink and stood, wobbling. She felt squiffy and climbed the stairs carefully, thinking about the delicious chicken, waiting to be cooked for Christmas dinner. It would be a good day; she could sense it. She would have a relaxing hot bath and be up early to get on with the Christmas Day preparations.

Clara waited until she heard Auntie May get in the bath, then crept downstairs. "Come on, Cyril," she whispered, "Don't make so much noise."

She opened a drawer in the dresser and took a knife. She held it up and ran her hand gently along its blade. Mmm, nice and sharp.

She tiptoed to the stairs; Cyril at her rear, egging her on. Without Auntie, she could run the pub with Cyril. They would be a happy family at last.

"Auntie?" she said, as she opened the bathroom door. "Happy Christmas."

Birds of a Feather

Mary Ogilvie

It's early. Very early, as I stretch after a good night's sleep. Gloria was moving about restlessly last night, but she's due to lay our eggs soon, so it's understandable. Then our lives will change. With young ones to take care of, it's not an easy task in any world.

The air is fresh. I like it at this time, when a new day begins. Peaceful, until the dawn chorus starts. Then, their din ruffles anybody's feathers. The thing is, those birds never have a day off, something which would be appreciated now and again.

Gliding through the water, I can see someone across at the water's edge, and a dog comes into view. It's the start of the dog walkers' brigade. Dogs can be threatening, so it's best to keep at a distance.

I look back at Gloria. She seems more settled and peaceful now, so it's time for my breakfast before she wants hers. Going into deeper water, I enjoy my first meal of the day – food being plentiful in these rich waters.

Some of the others are beginning to stir from their slumber, and I set sail to catch up on the latest news. Just then I notice Henrietta Heron: her usual tall, elegant self, motionless in the reed bed on the edge of the pool. Henrietta has the patience of a saint as she watches and waits for any unsuspecting prey that catches her attention. And there is plenty, so she's never short of a meal or two.

I spot Jeffrey swimming without his partner, Mildred. They have been courting for a while, but now that they have a young family, it's over to her to hold the reins. During their courtship, he was devoted to her. Never left her side, especially when she was being pursued by two other male admirers. These mallard ducks make me smile.

But talking of courtship, we have a star performance from the great crested grebe in the spring. With chestnut and black frills around its head, it looks the part, with its head shaking, diving and dancing out of the water. It's applause all round and an occasion not to miss.

Swimming on, I greet my friend, Samuel the coot. "Hi there, how are you?" I enquire, as I drift closer to him.

"Oh, not so good, Charles. I have a poorly stomach."

"Not a fishing hook, I hope. Sometimes anglers can be so careless."

"No, just something I've eaten," Samuel assures me.

I nod and understand. People come to the water's edge to feed us, with bags of bread mainly. It fills, and is gratefully received, especially in leaner times when food is scarcer to find. But sometimes, just sometimes, it can be something different, inedible. And that's when the trouble starts.

"Glad to hear that, Samuel," I say, and off I go.

Out of the corner of my eye I notice, almost hidden in the bushes by the bank, a long face with bright eyes looking out. "Good morning, Larry Fox," I call out.

Knowing he's been spotted, he turns tail and disappears. Another arch enemy to watch out for, especially with little ones about.

The sun is beginning to break through, and I feel the warmth on my body. It's going to be a heavenly day. By now, the cries of gulls break the tranquillity and make their presence felt. Always on the lookout for scraps, they are a noisy bunch and have no etiquette at all.

It's the same with the Canada geese. They come here to escape the harsher winter weather in the northern climes. But they parade around with their heads held high, making their honking sound as if they own the place. And just when you are used to having them around, without a by your leave, they are off. Charming!

Walter and Victoria, our resident pair of tufted ducks, are a perfect example of wildlife on the pond. They dive for their dinner, mind their own business and never gossip. They don't like all the hassle of visitors dropping in and out. They prefer a quieter life. It's hard to please everyone.

But life here is good, sharing our home with so many species of insects and birds, including our friend Charlie the reed warbler – one of our drop-in visitors. Although I haven't seen or heard Charlie this year. He's a small, cute, olive-brown bird with a chattering song. We usually find him perched on a reed stem by the edge of the pool and his familiar presence on our doorstep is welcomed. I hope he has come to no harm.

As I soak up the sun's rays, I can honestly say it's a pleasure to reside on this pool, even though there is the ever-present danger both from animal and man himself, who we hope will always treat us with respect. There is no overcrowding, and I understand it is the second largest expanse of water in Coventry.

It is such an extremely valuable habitat, supporting such a wide variety of water birds and pond life, and it also offers a winter stop for many migrating birds such as the snipe and shoveler. That reminds me. Patricia Snipe and her partner put in a visit to the pool when you least expect them. That long straight bill of hers helps to find worms and invertebrates in the mud. She's a darling and everyone's favourite.

43

Bill Shoveler's path crosses with Patricia's as he and his beloved drop in too. Such a duck, with that huge bill of his. He's hard to miss, but both are welcome.

As I look around the pool, our surroundings are magnificent, with tall grasses, meadowsweet and willowherb attracting insects and butterflies. The small wood and hedgerows nearby also attract wildlife, so we have a lot of birdsong and activity going on.

Occasionally you might see Philip the kingfisher, with his coat of azure blue. So small but stunning. He does not linger but prefers to reside on branches over the River Sowe, which flows around the edge of the reserve. You tend to hear his high-pitched whistle before you see him. But he adds to the scene with his beauty.

Billy the otter enjoys life with fellow friends in the River Sowe next door. He's mainly out and about at night so I don't get to see him much. He's a playful chap and enjoys nothing more than a meal of crayfish.

At dusk, before Gloria and I retire for the night, you can hear the sound of Percy the nocturnal water rail bird. He sounds like a piglet squealing and tends to skulk around the reed beds – but we know he's there.

Snapping out of my passive thinking, I notice a lady walking down the bank. She's wearing a green coat. She often comes to feed us, especially on cold days. She takes her time and talks to us.

"Well, Charles Swan, how are you today?" I hear her gentle voice.

How does she know my name? I glide closer and nibble some of her food, thankful for her care. I wonder about her. She seems to take such an interest in all around, and often sits and writes in a little book. It must be full by now, as she notes with darting eyes all that goes on.

Suddenly, I hear a familiar sound through the air and know it's Gloria calling me. I look at the lady and she tells me, "You're needed, Charles. It's time to go and welcome your next generation to the Stoke Floods Local Nature Reserve."

Air Transport Auxiliary

Derek Medcraft

Armstrong Whitworth Plant, Baginton, Coventry April 1942.

Basil tapped the intercom button on the telephone. "Karen, can you ask Mr Daly to come to my office now, please?"

Karen telephoned the workshop supervisor's office. "Bill, is Gerard with you?"

Bill looked through the window at the two-hundred-yard-long workshop. "No, but I can see him coming this way."

"Good, could you ask him to come to Mr Fellows' office immediately, please."

Ten minutes later Gerard approached Karen." Good morning, Karen. What's he want today?"

"I think you had better go straight in. He didn't get much sleep last night, with the Luftwaffe and the Air Ministry telephoning him."

"The Luftwaffe telephoned him?" said Gerard with a smirk.

"Gerard, stop teasing me. Remember, walls have ears – also sausages."

"Cor, I haven't had one of them for months." Gerard knocked and walked into Basil's office.

Basil was in his late fifties; six feet tall, slim with black hair, an olive complexion with dark brown eyes and a pencil moustache. As Gerard entered he rose from behind his desk and beckoned him further into his office.

Gerard was a couple of inches shorter and twenty years younger than Basil. He had brown hair, green eyes with a cheeky glint in them (obviously something he had inherited from his Irish parentage), a fashionable short back and sides haircut and a full beard.

"Gerard – good morning and get that mop shaved off or join the bloody navy."

"Is it, sir?"

"Is it what?"

"A good morning?"

"You know it isn't. We have this conversation every morning. Between the ministry and the Luftwaffe, no morning is ever good. Three o'clock this morning, the ministry were chasing me for aircraft – they think they grow on bloody trees."

"The navy, sir."

"Gerard, it may have escaped your attention but we build bombers – bloody great big Lancaster bombers – so what's the navy got to do with all this?"

"They won't have me sir. I tried – this is a reserved occupation and all that."

"Right, forget that. When's the next plane ready? I need to phone the ministry so they can get one of their Air Transport Auxiliary pilots down here to fly it out."

"Where's it going, sir?"

"Germany, I hope, but you know I'm not privy to that sort of information. Now find out when we'll have an aircraft ready."

"If the engines turn up in the next hour we'll have the plane on the runway by two o'clock this afternoon, so if they can get a pilot here for one o'clock for the pre-flight checks, everything should be tickety boo."

"Tickety boo," Basil said, rolling his eyes.
"I'll get the pilot here. You make sure you meet him at the gate and escort him here. I don't want any Tom, Dick or Harry wandering around this plant as and when they feel like it."

Gerard left the office and quietly closed the door. He looked at Karen and winked. "That wasn't so bad," he said.

"I'll get the gateman to hold the pilot there and I'll let you know when he's arrived."

"Thanks, Karen. I don't know what we would do without you."

Gerard went back to the workshop to check with Bill the workshop foreman that everything was running to schedule.

Some hours later, Bill answered the telephone. "It's for you, Gerard. The pilot's arrived and they're holding him at the gate with his motorbike."

"Tell them to send him straight up to the main office. We'll be there to meet him and we're not putting his motorbike in the bomb bay again – he can get the train back from wherever."

Bill and Gerard walked the length of the building, looking at each bomber as they passed, quickly noting what stage of build they were in and calculating when the next ones would be ready to fly.

The workforce was made up of men and women. Some were fitting the rear turrets while others were fitting and riveting fuselage panels, and wing panels top and bottom. Engine fitment was restricted to men: four per engine, sixteen men in total.

Bill and Gerard walked out of the main entrance just as the pilot was pulling a BSA M20 motorcycle back on its stand.

He turned to face them, wearing a leather helmet, goggles, a leather flying jacket over the top of a regulation green one-piece army issue boiler suit, leather flying boots and leather gauntlets.

Gerard looked at Bill and then back to the pilot, who stood four inches shorter than Gerard himself. He said, "You know it's a Lancaster bomber you're flying today?"

Just as he finished speaking the pilot removed her goggles and leather helmet and shook her head, letting her wavy auburn silky hair fall down to her shoulders.

Gerard took a half step back and looked into an open face with smooth skin, sparkling green eyes and a petite nose.

"Wow!" he uttered.

"My name is Rhonna Clements and I have just spent six hours at Castle Bromwich, waiting for a runway to be repaired so I could fly a Spitfire out. Then I receive a telegram telling me to report here. I've spent two hours on my motorbike, dodging bomb craters for twenty miles, and fifteen minutes at your gatehouse where they wanted to strip-search me."

"I bet they did," muttered Bill.

"And finally, when I do eventually get here I'm met by a pair of half-baked male chauvinists, who have nothing better to do than to stand in front of me with open mouths and utter futile exclamations like WOW!"

"He said that," said Bill, pointing at Gerard.

"Just... just send me to your leader so I can hand in my orders," said Rhonna, with an exasperated sigh.

Gerard opened the door for her and pointed to the top of the stairs. As Rhonna walked through the doors, he said, "My friends call me Ges."

"Thank you – I'll stick with Gerard if you don't mind," replied Rhonna.

"That told us two, didn't it? I'd better get that aircraft on the apron, otherwise I think she'll have our guts for garters," said Bill.

Rhonna met Mr Fellows and handed in her orders and identification papers. He made a phone call, came back and said, "Okay, everything tallies. I'll get Mr Daly to take you out to the aircraft. Karen, can you find Mr Daly please and tell him Miss Clements is waiting?"

"Where are you flying this beast to?" Basil enquired.

"Secret and confidential," she answered. "Is Mr Daly the gentlemen I met earlier?" she asked.

"Yes, he's a damned hard worker and he's not a chauvinist," replied Basil with a wink.

Rhonna smiled for the first time that day.

As Bill had promised, the huge beast stood outside the flight shed with all four Merlin engines roaring. The top half of the plane was painted with green and brown camouflage; the bottom half was painted black – a better colour for night-time bombing.

Gerard escorted Rhonna towards the aircraft and stopped a short distance away so she would hear what he had to say without the roar of the engines drowning him out. He carried with him a pack of sandwiches and a flask. Rhonna was carrying her helmet, goggles and gauntlets in her left hand. Gerard placed his left hand on her right forearm momentarily, stopping her.

Before Gerard could say anything, Rhonna said, "I owe you and your friend an apology."

Gerard smiled and said, "No, wait. This morning was a shock to me. I didn't realise I was looking into the face of the girl I'm going to marry. Now take these sandwiches and coffee and get into the cockpit."

"Coffee?"

"Yes, every Friday my mum gives me a flask of coffee."

Rhonna took her presents and walked towards the ladder leading into the aircraft. After a few yards she stopped, turned, smiled for the second time that day and shouted, "Ges, I think I'm going to like your mum."

Bill walked up behind Gerard and muttered into his ear. "She's quite feisty, isn't she?"

"Where's her motorbike?"

"In the bomb bay," replied Bill.

The Lancaster roared some more. Rhonna opened the cockpit window, leaned out and shouted, "I'll make sure you get your flask back."

The Lancaster started rolling down the runway, gathering speed. It took what seemed like an eternity for the tail wheel to lift; some ten seconds later the undercarriage wheels left the ground, and she was flying and gaining height every second.

Bill and Gerard turned to each other, laughed and walked back to the hangars.

Authors Note:

Lancaster bombers were built in Manchester, Birmingham and Coventry. The Air Transport Auxiliary was made up of men and women who flew all manner of aircraft, including Lancasters, from point of manufacture to their appropriate squadron.

Did Gerard and Rhonna get married? Well, I'll leave that to the reader's imagination.

The Light Pours Out

Ian Collier

In Coventry there is an inauspicious house. A mid-terrace, just
down behind the Holyhead Road to the west of the city centre,
where you'll now find the great-grandson of Arthur Hillman.
Arthur was a fairly normal man, but for his refusal to grow old.
That doesn't mean he refused to grow old gracefully or even
grow old disgracefully – he just refused to grow old.

Howard Hillman, his grandson, only inherited the house
after Arthur died in a road traffic incident. Atypically for a
centenarian, Arthur died while jogging. He died because he
failed to hear the car's horn and its screeching brakes above his
iPod. He'd only recently taken up jogging – some rumoured
that it was so he could keep up with his fifty-year-old
girlfriend, others said it was so he could stay ahead of her and
still have a bit on the side. Howard wished to be like Arthur,
willing to give anything to be so alive for so long.

There were two things that people often said about
Arthur. The first, which was ironic considering his longevity,
was that he lived fast: he drank to excess, he smoked, he'd
never been faithful to any of his wives, but he had always
avoided violence. That was incredible for someone who had a
worse reputation for entertaining bored housewives than a
brigade of Dairy Crest's finest. The second thing was more a
feeling than an observation: he didn't seem whole, as though
some tiny but essential part of his being was missing. Some
people claimed that he drank to fill a hole, others that he drank
to forget it. The women were there to distract him from

thinking of it, but always people felt there was that gap in his core.

Then there was the house again. It didn't appear special; horological touches had been chiselled into the sandstone of the lintels and sills; eccentric yet not exceptional. During the blitz Arthur had refused to leave the house while bombs rained down. As a firestorm swept the neighbouring streets, his row of houses was barely singed. One of the fire-fighters swore that the sparks flying towards the row glowed white briefly, then floated to the ground with grey wisps of smoke trailing like a comet's tail. A bomb went through the roof of the end terrace. When the disposal men finally got to it the timer was rusted solid and the explosives had deteriorated to impotency.

Arthur, when the police finally marched him to the recruitment board, was rejected. In theory he worked in a reserved profession in one of the aero-engine factories, but what saved him was his irregular heartbeat that sometimes got as fast as 220 beats a minute or as low as zero.

Arthur had trained in watches before becoming a tool maker for Armstrong's. The house, fittingly, was an old watchmaker's house with a workshop built out at the back, over the kitchen. Unlike the rest of the row, it still had the big windows, allowing in maximal light – something that would only be observed by those who knew to look. The front of the house had seen its sash windows replaced with aluminium and, more recently, uPVC double glazing. Throughout the inside it had been modernised and upgraded, but the workshop was somehow untouched.

That was something Howard decided to rectify. He didn't want to move to this side of town but, with a little investment, the house would turn from a two-bedroom into a three-, with the workshop becoming a walk-through study and

53

a bathroom. That should increase the value by at least thirty grand when it went up for sale.

Howard set to work almost before the banana his granddad had left in the workshop could ripen – in fact as soon as the soil had settled onto the coffin.

The first job was to measure up, which is where the initial confusion set in – there were about three metres missing. Howard measured the kitchen and found it longer than the room exactly above it. Time always seemed to run differently around that house, but now space became a variable too. He soon figured out that from the end of the huge window to the back wall was where the deficiency lay.

The first part of the renovation had to be clearing out the junk. Small machines of every description were flashed onto eBay. Watchmakers' lathes, corroded brass mechanisms, hand-painted faces: all saw frantic bidding; about the only thing he couldn't sell was a bunch of keys.

With the space clear, he could start to pull out the workbench – only that didn't go as expected. Hammers seemed to slow down as they swung downwards, losing rather than gaining momentum. They impacted so slowly that they made no impression. Saws rusted and their teeth crumbled; the bench wasn't going anywhere. A closer inspection showed that there were no angle brackets, so the bench went through the misplaced wall rather than being fastened to it. In Howard's mind there was only one option: attack the wall.

He tapped until he found a part that sounded hollow. This revealed a door-shaped section in the middle of the wall, hidden from view by layers of paper. As with the bench, outright violence didn't work – tools broke or failed to function. But he found a wallpaper scraper effective and it gradually revealed a flat wooden door, set flush into a smooth,

54

plastered wall. After blunting several drill bits he started working through the keys he'd failed to sell, eventually finding the right one. With a click, the door was free and jerked towards him.

He pulled it back and looked inside. At the other end of the indestructible workbench sat a wizened old man, bald and grey-skinned to the point where he actually seemed to radiate a grime-filled light. In his gnarled hand a large clock key trembled against the side of a monstrous carriage clock. Its pendulum swung intermittently: stopping, starting, accelerating and slowing down at random throughout its stroke. Its second hand whizzed round and then appeared to stop.

The minute hand didn't move as Howard stood there; however, behind him in the workshop, shadows grew long and the sunlight was replaced by sodium yellow.

Just before dawn, the old man finished his rotation and faced Howard. There was something of Arthur about him, only frailer than a worm-riddled corpse. His only hint of colour was the bloated nose, where the veins showed a faint purple through the grey skin. The eyes glinted with recognition – or it could have been relief, as he threw the clock key to his newly cursed grandson?

He wheezed, "Young Howard? If you're here then I assume I'm dead."

Instinctively Howard snatched at the flying key and in that moment, that second, that millennium, he stopped being one Howard. A part of him brushed the dust from where Arthur had sat; the other slammed the door of the workshop and then that of the house, as he headed out to get very, very drunk.

Coundon Dreams

M. A. Forster

Sometimes these incidents just happen. But not to me. Not normally. I am walking, a stranger in my city, when the whiff of a long-forgotten smell comes to my nose. Then a sudden noise, poking at a memory that isn't mine.

I am walking in the lower parts of Coundon, the area where I grew up. Except it isn't 'my' Coundon anymore.

Coundon House, once a building of delight and mystery to a child who played school sports on the grass before it, has been converted into flats. More flats encroach onto its proud past. Hell, even the grass field, once part of the estate's lawns, has been built upon. And behind it, the school where I learned about the planets and Tolkein, dinosaurs and Romans until the age of eleven, has been demolished.

Generally, the houses and roads, built on much of the former Coundon House land, are the same as in my childhood. Well, not quite the same. Once-proud homes show signs of neglect and despair. Gardens paved over for cars, or pebbled over for effect.

Entries are overgrown, looking pitifully back at me from behind their modern incarceration.

But on to Coundon Road. Where it happened. The old wooden clinic where my childhood ailments were tackled stands behind more bars. Forgotten, rotting, the ghosts of memories trapped inside.

Dismayed at the way we have treated our history, my mood dips further as I pass the identikit apartments that crowd the erstwhile field of dreams 'next door'. Where top

56

internationals strode a stage fit for the kings of the oval ball game. The greats played here in the days when Coventry was great, when Peter Jackson set matches alight with his mercurial magic. And then his heir, David Duckham, in a back division that boasted the guile, speed and sabre-like running of fellow England internationals Webb, Rossborough, Preece and Evans.

The 'luxury' apartments are already showing the signs of wear and tear. Poor substitute.

I shake my head and continue to Coundon Road station. It closed before I was born, but looms large in the history of my family – Coundon folk since the 1920s. It was here they caught trains to visit family in Longford, my great-grandmother joking with the station master that she wanted 'one and a half to Abergavenny'.

The station house remains, transformed into a building for the neighbouring grammar school. Everything else was swept away in the hysteria following Dr Richard Beeching's infamous report. The platforms are crumbling, overgrown with vegetation. Trains still rumble past, but smaller in length and fewer in number.

The signal box, a monument to a past when it controlled nearly twenty lines of goods yard, still stands forlornly redundant. The goods yard, where black gold from the collieries came to heat several generations of homes, schools and businesses, has disappeared under more identikit homes.

I stand on the crossing, considering Coventry's dismal decline and the crux of my dreams to be an author. Or my doom to be a dreamer.

Those wistful thoughts include Coundon House, a fantasy to be written. Involving the tall, impressive homes on the city-side – we always called the city 'town' – of the railway line. Victorian homes of grandeur for the rich and

57

famous, the up-and-coming, when allotment gardens, farms and even a brickworks stood on the Coundon side of the crossing.

Those homes have been turned into yet more flats and bedsits, care homes and places to deposit some of life's undesirables.

I don't move for a while. Instead I stand, staring. Remembering. Dreaming. East, west, north and south. At the old Carbodies site, where tens of thousands of black cabs have been churned out in a lifetime.

Yes, I grew up in Coundon, immersed in its social history and my family's history.

I remembered the underpass, built in the same stone as the station house and the retaining walls for the former goods yard. The same stone that is visible further along towards town, at the junction where the gas yard, now completely erased from history, stood, and St Osburg's towered.

The railway had come in the 1840s. Unwelcome. Mistrusted. Linking parts of the city that already existed when Coundon, as it became, didn't. When it was a tiny village a mile and a half away. Farming country. Before the grammar school.

An out-of-town development.

But Coundon was growing. Enough for the underpass to be built in the early 1860s. So I walk there and stand underneath the arched stone. Treading on cobbles unchanged in a century and more.

I smile. I think of the story I am writing and imagine this place when it was newly-built.

Until the smell. What is it? Steam? From a train? Can't be. And that noise? An odd clunking from somewhere nearby. I grew up here, know its sounds, but…

58

I must have been dreaming, for the homes have gone and in the middle distance is a tall chimney, which somehow I know is the brick-making plant. And here, instead of railwaymen's cottages, are allotment gardens. And I can't believe it, but two men in black uniforms and caps are standing by the closed wicket gates of the crossing as a locomotive I somehow know is a Cauliflower, in the blackberry colours of the London and North Western Railway, slowly pulls to a stop.

Strange. I know the LNWR ceased to exist in 1923.

Three coaches behind the tender shimmy to a halt by the pristine, weed-free platforms. I stand, as transfixed as I was minutes earlier. I realise there are allotments on the other side of the line, too. No grammar school. That was built in the early 1890s.

The big houses town-side are there though, dominant and proud. And here, walking along the platform, is a man who looks the spitting image of the character I have invented for my Coundon fantasy. Coming to meet me...

Coventry Born and Bred I am

By Derek Medcraft

"Where do you come from?" enquired the stranger.
Not far from here; I'll give you a clue.

The city was here long before me and you.
Some say the name was derived from a convent,
others a coffer tree,
and there are spires of three, that's true.

There was ribbon making and weaving,
watches and leather goods, too.
Some say True Blue was here before you,
and Godiva rode through.

It's said the city's given a lot to the world:
Wickmans, Herberts, Standard Triumph,
Jaguar, Rolls Royce –
just to mention a few.

Massey Ferguson, Dunlop and Rootes:
young and old had a hand in these.
All round the world their goods were hurled,
and all were sold, meaning jobs unfurled.
Their skills were core and much more.

It's reputed the rugby was good here, too.
Duckham, Preece and Evans, that's who
played the Red Rose, these men of Coventry Blue.
Don't forget Rossborough, Webb and Cotton too.
All these I remember as being true.

Not so long ago, the football was just as good.
In the top tier of England our heroes stood.
The finest game the FA had seen.
Three goals to two when the whistle blew,
and the city roared at every goal scored.
I know that to be true.

Coventry born and bred, that's me.
And very proud of it too – that's true!

Memories of a Munchkin

Margaret Mather

"I said no, Henry, and I am not going to say it again. How many times do I have to tell you? There will be thousands of people there, you won't be able to get near, and it'll be dangerous. I'll take you to Walsgrave, but I am not, and neither are you, going into the city centre tomorrow. Do I make myself clear?"

I was twelve years of age; my senses had been awoken to the joy of football and an intense love affair with Coventry City followed. Through thick and thin, good and bad, fat and lean times, wherever they went, I followed. I watched them win in the semi-finals and afterwards the city erupted with flag-waving, music blaring and car drivers beeping their horns. People were joyous; they had an air of expectation about them, something to look forward to. That was the day when everyone in Coventry thought – yes, this is real, and we could win the FA Cup.

The big day dawned; the date forever etched in my memory. 16th May 1987, Coventry City's first ever FA Cup final. Mum had tried to get tickets but they were like gold dust, and I had to make do with watching it at my friend Glen's house. His dad and some other friends were there. Women, he said, were barred. Mum told me to behave; in hindsight I think she should have told Glen's dad to behave. We were shouting at the television, jumping on the chairs and waving our scarves and flags every time Coventry came near the ball. We gave the ref a hard time and I learned some new words. It was a mad ninety minutes; then we were in extra time. Everyone held their breath for the rest of the game. When we won 3–2, Coventry exhaled and turned sky blue. Car horns were blaring. Everywhere you looked there were sky blue flags, sky blue scarves; we even saw a man painting his front door sky blue.

We jumped on a bus going into town and the driver said the ride was free. We laughed all the way to the city centre; a real carnival atmosphere surrounded us.

"Where have you been, Henry? It's 9.30pm and I've been frantic with worry," Mum said.

"Glen's dad took us for a pizza to celebrate and I couldn't find a phone that was working."

Just a small white lie. I had to touch my nose to make sure I was not in a Pinocchio moment.

"Next time, you make sure you come home before wandering off. Do you understand, Munchkin?" (Mum's pet name for me and I hated it.)

"Yes Mum."

"Now, up to bed – we need to be up early tomorrow to bag a good spot."

It was times like these that a boy needed his father. Unfortunately my father had gone off with the lady who lived across the road and we were now a single-parent family.

"Fur coat and no knickers, that one," Mum would say to our next-door neighbour as she nodded her head at the house across the way.

The next day I was up at 6 o'clock. We found a great place to stand on the roundabout at Walsgrave. There were loads of people, all in good humour, all wearing blue. A cheer the likes of which I had never heard before arose from the crowd when the bus and players appeared. The team responded by taking it in turns to hold the cup aloft so that everyone could see. It was a fantastic, jaw-dropping, heart-stopping moment and I wanted more.

It was then that I thought, "I want to be where the action is."

I hatched a plan and knew that I'd have to act calm and indifferent, otherwise my mother would know that something was going on. When we returned home I asked if I could call for Glen.

"OK," she said, "be back for dinner at two. Do not under any circumstances go to town."

I nodded, but knew that I wasn't going to let this day pass without heading for the city to see my heroes again.

Glen and I walked into town, the crowds and euphoria carrying us high on a tidal wave of happiness. Just as we passed the Lady Godiva statue, a man dressed from head to foot in blue was trying to mount the horse. He fell off and landed in the crowd. Everyone laughed. The nearer we got to the Council House, the denser it became. People were pushing and shoving, all trying to get the best vantage point. They were sitting on top of roofs, astride bridges and up lampposts. Glen was feeling a bit claustrophobic and he looked a little on the pale side. I thought, any minute now he'll throw up.

Just then, a man who was up one of the lampposts and could see what was happening hauled Glen out of the crowd and up onto the lamppost. Glen's shoe fell off and someone picked it up and started to use it as a football, mimicking yesterday's match. It looked like Glen had lost his shoe for good; I didn't know how he would explain that to his mother.

I lost sight of Glen as I was carried along by the crowd. We came to a standstill on Pepper Lane and couldn't get any further. Mum had been right when she said I wouldn't be able to see anything. I hadn't come this far, disobeying my mother in the process, not to be able to see them. Suddenly a police car wove its way through the crowd. Tucking myself behind its wake, I managed to get outside the balcony where the team were. A very proud moment for me.

It was late when I got home. Mum was furious. "Where've you been? I was just about to call the police."

"I'm sorry, Mum. Glen fell and broke his arm. I had to go to hospital with him, and because of the crowds it took forever to get there. The hospital was very busy. I tried to call but lost my money in the phone box." (Another Pinocchio moment.)

I was sorry for putting Mum through this, but not sorry about the best day of my life.

"That's you grounded for a month, Harry. I'll pop down and see Glen tomorrow."

Oh no – I would just have to worry about that tomorrow. Today belonged to the Sky Blues.

I'm 38 now and still remember that weekend as if it were yesterday. It's a shame Coventry City Football Club have landed up in the mess they're in today. I still go with my son. We hope against hope that their fortunes will turn, and we blame everyone from the board to the managers to the players for Coventry City's demise.

I can only pray that the Sky Blues will return to their former glory, and my son will one day experience the joy I did when we won the FA Cup.

My mother, to this day, still calls me Munchkin.

Everything but the Book:
The Tale of an Aspiring Coventry Author

Rosalie Warren

Three publishers are interested: they've lined up in a queue;
nine agents want to see my work: they loved my overview.
I've two pages up on Facebook – one for me, one for the book;
I'm blogging three times daily – oh won't you take a look?
My characters are tweeting like a noisy flock of wrens;
I have T-shirts for publicity, a mug and ninety pens.
They've my details printed on them – I'd a special photo done;
It's costing me a fortune but I'm having so much fun!

I stand outside the Ricoh to accost the football fans;
I thrust pens and mugs and business cards into their sweaty
hands.
I've given talks in libraries, in prisons and in schools;
I've done interviews in bookshops, by canals, in swimming
pools...
I'm up to date on income tax; I know my copyrights;
my cover blurb is perfect and the Booker's in my sights.
I'm all signed up for PLR – or is it PLO?
I've a pen-name and a bank account – just let that money flow!

A guy responded to my blog – he said he'd tout my book;
I gave him thirteen hundred pounds – sadly, he was a crook.
But I'm soldiering on undaunted – I subscribe to Writing Mag;
I've read every book on 'How to' from Will Empson to Jo
Bragg.
My head is full of P.O.V; I've joined the SoA;
I'm a regular at festivals, from Keswick down to Hay.
I'm up to scratch on all the latest market swings and trends;
I've met lots of famous authors – some of them are even
'friends'!

My Writers'-n-Artists' Yearbook is stained with coffee
grounds,
with chocolate smears on publishers who've dared to turn me
down.
My characters' proclivities are typed up in a list
and I even know the toenail length of my protagonist.
My dialogue is flawless; I always stick to 'said';
my metaphors are never mixed, my 'darlings' killed stone
dead.
I'm a master of the cliff-hanger, the turning point and hook...
now all I have to do is go and write the bloody book!

Sent to Coventry

Margaret Egrot

In February 2013, hundreds of hopefuls queued in sub-zero temperatures outside a nightclub in the city centre, for a chance to audition for a role in the proposed reality TV show – 'Sent to Coventry'. Forty-something Kelley from the King's Arms was one of them.

Jesus, its cold out here. Talk about freezing the balls off a brass monkey! Kevin said I should wear my parka, but who wants to look like Mum on the school run on a day like this? Not that he wanted me to get on the show, mind. For all we could do with the publicity, he said it would be embarrassing for him with his mates. And what would his mum say?

"Well," I said, "your mum thinks I'm dirt anyway, so her opinion of me couldn't sink any lower. But think of what it would do for the pub if I did get on. It's bound to bring in more custom."

The new knockers are wasted on our regulars, I told him. Sad old geysers with watery eyes who order half pints and make them last all evening. Pub's dying on its feet – I'm doing it for the business really. Though I'm not saying I wouldn't be tempted by a proper career in show business afterwards.

I've been here nearly an hour and the queues hardly moved. My feet are like lumps of ice. Maybe I should have just whipped my top off. Some brassy piece did just that and Security rushed across and took her straight in. She'll be auditioning now, I'll bet. But I'll tell you this for free – her bombers aren't anything like as big as mine. Bit saggy too.

And her roots were showing. At least I bothered to get mine done beforehand. No point flashing your new carumbas if the rest of you's not up to snuff.

Same goes for that chap in a fluorescent thong thingy. Ten out of ten for pluck, I'll give him that – but all he's done is show the world what a paunch he's got – and hairs on his back too. Eugh! All he'll get out of this is a nasty chill. Silly bugger.

The woman in front of me has brought a dog – says it's the dog that's auditioning, not her. Huge great beast and he looks as bored as hell. I wonder if I could bunch up a bit and get my feet under his belly to warm them up. Oh, perhaps not! I don't like the look of those teeth, and his mistress is baring hers too now. Best keep my distance.

I'll agree with Kev on one thing: six inch heels aren't made for standing still in, platforms or no platforms. I wouldn't have worn them, only they put me over six foot, and they do help throw your marimbas forward when you walk. Kinda sexy, you know? Essex-way, like. That – and the tan.

The judges will be nice and warm in there. Probably on to their second coffee by now. Maybe third. Anyway, at least we've moved forward a bit in the last few minutes. At this rate I should be in before it gets really dark.

They want people on the show who are larger than life – a bit Jeremy Kyle, they said. Well, there's a few like that in this city, if the rumpus behind me is anything to go by. Sounds like Security are in business again – only this time they're taking the trouble-makers away from the building. Being too mouthy never works. Not that I was tempted. I'll get in on my talent. My dad always said I had an artistic temperament. Kevin calls it being a show-off, but he doesn't understand what it is to be sensitive. I wonder if he's remembered to Hoover the bar.

It's so bloody freezing; you wouldn't think spring is just around the corner. Even my nipples are cold – sticking out like raspberries under my blouse, I shouldn't wonder.

I'm going to sing – see if it'll take my mind off my numb muchachas.

[Sings] "Why are we waiting...?"

Well, that's got everyone going – and it's taking my mind off my effing feet as well. A spot of dancing before I turn into a stala... stala... what's-it might help too. Come on, girls and boys – let's get a bit of Zumba going whilst we've got time to kill. Ah, that's more like it.

Five o'clock and the sun's gone down. I wouldn't have believed it could get any colder – by my reckoning a monkey wouldn't have any balls left to freeze if it were here. Makes me feel sorry for the homeless, this weather. We did a quiz once at the pub to raise money for Shelter. That's when business was a bit better than it is now. The way we're going it'll be me and Kev in a shop doorway in a few months.

Queue's moving a bit faster at last. At this rate I should be at the head of the queue by six o'clock, six-fifteen tops. Perhaps they've got a better idea of what they're looking for. Or perhaps they've already made their choices and are just going through the motions. God, I really hope not. Best touch my slap up now to be ready. Just a bit of lippy. I don't need any more powder – sweating's the least of my problems today.

What's happening now with the people at the front? Someone has come out to talk to them. Whatever it is, they don't like it. Fists flying. Christ! I wouldn't like to have been on the receiving end of that one. And here comes Security again. It's a real ding-dong. Well, if they send that lot packing, I'll be in even sooner.

70

What's that? The audition's closed? No! But they haven't seen me yet. They can't do that – it's not fair. They've got to see me... Listen, love, you tell them – I can sing, I can dance, I get on with people, I'm feisty, I've got great tits... No, hear me out, will you? You get me in and I'll give you... Well I don't really know what I can give you, apart from a free drink. Oh, come on, guys! Give me a break, will you? I really, really need this... Well I'm going in anyway. I haven't stood eight hours in the sodding cold just to be treated like scum, so get out of my flipping way... Hey! Take your hands off me. Stop pushing... Ouch! All right, I'm going. Just let me get my shoe back on...

And an effing good night to you too.

That's it, then?

No audition.

No contract.

No show.

No name in bright lights.

So much for getting the pub back in the black.

What am I going to tell Kevin?

Daniel Pelka

Rosalie Warren

Shadows of two monsters leer from his urine-soaked mattress.
Daniel, small boy
from our city;
We adults, meant to care for you, have let you down.
We are so sorry.

1st August 2013

Free Christmas eBook offer

To say thank you for purchasing this book, we are offering you a free copy of our eBook, *Christmas Tales*. Available to read on your smartphone, eBook reader, tablet or PC, *Christmas Tales* consists of a number of short stories and poems on a seasonal theme, written by members of the Coventry Writers' Group.

Christmas Tales is available to buy from Amazon and iTunes, but it is available free to you. To download your free copy, visit:

www.smashwords.com/books/view/113914

About the Coventry Writers' Group

The Coventry Writers' Group was founded in the 1960s. We are the oldest established writing group in Coventry. Our group has always been supportive to anyone who has an interest in writing, and we welcome everyone, from complete beginners to professional writers.

Our meetings tend to be friendly, informal affairs, with lots of conversation about writing topics. We meet on the first Tuesday of each month. Our present meeting place is the Broomfield Tavern, Broomfield Place, Spon End, Coventry, at 8pm.

The Coventry Writers' Group meetings generally alternate by concentrating on readings of our work one month, and a workshop or speaker the following month.

We have always enjoyed real mix of members, from those just starting out with their writing ambitions, to those who are published in all forms of writing – poetry, plays, non-fiction, children's fiction, adult fiction, sci-fi, romance, magazine writing – all sorts.

In 2011 the Coventry Writers' Group put together and published an anthology of their work, called Coventry Tales. It became the best-selling book in Coventry that Christmas and went on to be awarded the Best Writers' Circle Anthology 2012. A second anthology – Christmas Tales – followed in eBook form.

For the last two years the group have also taken part in the Coventry Literary Festival, by putting on a performance of our work at the Criterian Theatre Earlsdon.

Membership of the Coventry Writers' Group is only £10 per year, and new members can enjoy three visits to see if it's for them before parting with any cash!

If you enjoy writing, whatever your genre, get in touch with us, or just turn up to one of our events. We look forward to meeting you.

www.CoventryWritersGroup.co.uk

www.facebook.com/groups/CoventryWritersGroup

Lightning Source UK Ltd.
Milton Keynes UK
UKOW04f0609061213

222442UK00002B/11/P